Sixth Grade Embalming

Brigit DiPrimo

ISBN:
ISBN-13:

Dedication

To all the students that have had a profound
impact on my life; especially Christian, and
with
thanks to my family, friends, and students over
the years for believing in me.

Contents

Chapter 1
Sixth Grade: Beginning of the End

~

Ms. Tincot was thought to be one of the coolest teachers, but also one of the most difficult. As luck would have it, I found myself in her class for sixth grade. I'm one of those kids who walks around with a label attached to them - you know what I mean. They might as well have a tattooed a sign on my forehead that says "troublemaker." It's not that I *try* to cause trouble, it just kind of happens. I know that sounds like a major cop-out, but it's true! Wherever I go, trouble is sure to follow. For example, the time in third grade when I decided to test the theory that the mashed "potatoes" in the cafeteria were, in fact, more like glue. By using them on a collage for my history class. What I saw as not only scientific but resourceful, my teacher saw as "inappropriate behavior." I was immediately sent to the principal and then to the social worker for an evaluation. And guess what? The photos I used in that collage are still perfectly affixed to the construction paper today. Turns out that I was completely correct in my assessment of the mysterious cafeteria substance.

Another incident sure to go down in any collection of our elementary school's darkest days would be the time I trimmed my eyebrows with a pair of scissors in second grade. I admit, it was not my brightest moment, but I was only trying to test their sharpness before using them. I was working on an intricate geometry project, and those shapes needed to be cut with a lot of care! But my teacher once again failed to see eye-to-eye with me, even though I was just taking pride in my work.

Every year, I entered school thinking that everything would be okay, and that my next teacher wouldn't know about my troubled history. This, of course, was never the case. Teachers seem to spend all their free time in the faculty lounge, discussing which kids are desirable and *un*desirable to have in class. I knew Ms. Tincot had a reputation for being able to handle the difficult kids, so I figured she had already formed her opinion of me by the time she saw my name on her class list. It's difficult to stroll into class with a positive, upbeat attitude when you feel the teacher already knows you're trouble, so on the first day of sixth grade, I entered the classroom a lot like a little kid gets into a dentist's chair - cautiously. I had to be ready for the oral surgeon and her dental team, AKA Ms. Tincot and my new classmates. I tried my best not to make any eye contact on my way in, but Ms. Tincot was not to be deterred from greeting each student, me included.

"Hey Christian, welcome to sixth grade! We're going to have a great year!" Sure, she acted excited, but I knew there was a bit of an edge to her voice. The only thing worse than a teacher who knows your reputation is one who knows and tries to hide it - but two could play at that game. I fired back with my standard first-day-of-school response: "I'm happy to be here." I was accustomed to blurting out standard phrases like that, and I thought it sounded convincing enough... though I was worried it might just seem pathetic.

I had no idea how different this year would be. My entire life was about to change. Forever.

Chapter 2
Ms. Tincot: Friend or Foe?

~

As I took my seat, I noticed several of my classmates from last year. They were whispering and shooting me looks. Not so much in a "Hey guys, look, we have Christian in our class again this year!" way, or a "Isn't it great to see him again?" way... more of a "Great, another year with the troublemaker" way. Just another common occurrence that I'd become all too familiar with. I'd mostly numbed myself to this sort of reaction, after spending 6 long years of my elementary school career with kids and teachers alike who I'd been told just didn't "get me."

Ms. Tincot seemed rather oblivious to the whispering boys and began to write something on the whiteboard. "These are some of the subjects that you will be studying this year", she announced. Hopefully, some of you will find one or more of these topics interesting and may even grow to like some of them. Sounds weird, I know." I liked the way she spoke to the class. It reminded me a bit of how I usually interacted with people. Some people took my sarcasm the wrong way, but people that really knew me, understood that it is my natural defense mechanism.

I decided it would look really good if I opened my notebook and copied down what was written on the board. Also known as "trying to gain brownie points with the teacher." A little brown nosing never hurt anyone. I had the feeling that once again she might have been on to me when I noticed her staring quizzically in my direction. I tried to act cool about it, but I'm not sure that's how it came off. "Mr. Mandow, are you currently working on your next great novel?" Ms. Tincot questioned. "Um... no, Ms. Tincot. I was simply making sure that I copied down all of the information on the immensely engaging subjects we will be learning about this year," I remarked.

After the words had already left my lips, I realized it was probably not one of my brighter responses. It was one of those instances where sarcasm was sure to paint me in a negative light in the teacher's eyes. I proceeded to turn the color of a raspberry and shrunk back into my chair. "Mr. Mandow, just how do you expect to find out about all of these 'immensely engaging' subjects with an attitude like that? Ms. Tincot remarked. That of course, was a good question. I had no answer.

Ms. Tincot let me off easy by letting the matter drop and going on with the rest of her introduction to the thrilling subjects of sixth grade. As I looked around the room, I could tell that one thought we probably all had in common was the thought that summer had ended far too soon, and homework was about to become our nightly visitor. Homework. Who on Earth invented such a means of torture? It makes no sense to be in school for countless hours only to be bringing more of that work home. I think I may have grounds for a lawsuit based on the school invading my privacy. The only thing saving me today was the traditional "first day of school dinner" my parents made every year.

For some reason, they would always leave work early on the first day of school to go shopping together to make a special dinner for me. I guess it was their way of trying to make me feel better. It did work a little bit because I always looked forward to it. As the bell rang to signal recess, I was brought back to the reality that the day was not yet over and playground politics were about to begin. A dance I knew all too well.

Chapter 3
Ryan: Friend

~

Social situations had never been easy for me. I always felt like people were talking about me, looking at me, or trying to "figure" me out. All of which I didn't particularly like. One person I could always count on to get me through these uncomfortable situations was my best friend, Ryan.

It seemed as though Ryan and I were separated at birth. We both loved playing video games, we both had a great affection for cats, and we carried the same "trouble-maker" label invisibly stamped on our foreheads by previous elementary school teachers. Ryan and I had never found ourselves in the same class, but we always managed to find each other on the playground which I was really hoping would be true today.

As I scoped the playground for any sign of Ryan, my eyes were suddenly drawn to a strange carving in the oak tree that had been on the playground ever since I had started Kindergarten. There was no way this carving had been here in previous years. I had walked the same path searching for Ryan year and after year and always passed this tree without noticing any strange carving. As I looked closer at the symbol carved into the tree, I noticed a shape that seemed to be reflective when the sun shone directly on it. It seemed as if the carving were done in pure gold. Must be some new-fangled pen one of the rich kids used to vandalize nature. I could not take my eyes off of the carving as I traced the outline with my pointer finger. I swear it began to glow. I quickly pulled my hand away and the glow subsided. This could not be happening. I hadn't even had lunch yet so there was no blaming the cafeteria food. I didn't feel particularly sick, I had slept well the night before and didn't notice any strange odor in the classroom that would account for this odd hallucination. I decided it must have been a trick the sunlight was playing on me.

I lifted my finger and placed it just above the part of that carving that resembled some sort of a bird. The bird began to turn god and glow with such an intensity that I had to look away in order to avoid being blinded. This was really happening. I had my doubts as to whether or not any students in the school would be sophisticated enough to make such a detailed carving and rig up some fancy electrical system that would allow an explanation for this. I decided that it was very possible that someone was playing a trick on me. There were certainly enough jokesters here that might like to get back at me for something I did in the past. For fear of embarrassment, I walked away and continued my search for Ryan. My mind however, stayed fixed on the carving in the tree.

While scanning the playground, I began to feel a strange sensation in my left arm. As I looked down, I noticed there was a mark slowly forming on the underside of my arm just above my wrist. I watched in horror as the mark became more and more noticeable. It couldn't be. I really have finally lost it, I thought to myself. I had to use every ounce of self-discipline I had to keep myself from screaming in fear of the image becoming clearer on my arm. "Woah....man, you got a tattoo?" Ryan shrieked. Then everything went black.

Chapter 4
Strange Symbols Begin

~

Upon awakening, I found myself lying flat on a cot in the nurse's office. Peering down at me were several fuzzy figures. One I recognized as Mr. Mandley, the nurse, the other Ryan. Mr. Mandley placed a cold compress on my forehead and made several tisking sounds signaling his pity for what had happened. Ryan spoke first in a caring tone. "Chris, man, how are you feeling?" I really wasn't sure how to answer him considering that I didn't even realize if this were a dream or not.

"I...feel....fine." I managed to whisper. I started playing through the events on the playground over and over in my mind in search of some reasonable explanation of what had happened out there. Mr. Mandley went back to his desk and picked up the phone, presumably to call my mother. "What in the world happened out there Ry?" I said pleadingly.

"I'm honestly really not sure man. I was looking all over the place and couldn't find you anywhere. When I finally did, you looked like you had seen a ghost and I noticed some weird mark on your arm. You seemed to be staring at it in some sort of a trance." Ryan remarked. I looked down at my left arm where I had seen the strange design appear and nothing remained. Maybe it was the right arm I thought. I turned over my right arm. Nothing.

"Ryan, what arm was that symbol on?" I begged.

"Um... your left arm I think"

"YOU THINK! This is no time to be unsure Ryan!" I yelled.

As the words left my mouth, I realized I was now completely freaking out. Ryan looked at me as if I were some sort of insane person and then walked over to Mr. Mandley. I couldn't hear what they were saying but I have a feeling it was something like, "Christian has finally gone completely insane. It's time to call the mental hospital and have him committed." I was feeling a lot better physically and decided it was time to try and get up and find some answers.

"Woah....hold on there cowboy. Where do you think you're going?" barked Mr. Mandley.

"I feel fine. I need to go back to class." I said. I headed for the door only to be met by Ryan blocking the exit. "Ryan, I am fine. Get out of the way!"

"I don't think so. Your mom is on her way and you need to lay down and rest until then." said Ryan. Great, I thought to myself. How am I possibly going to explain these strange occurrences to my mother? She will probably freak out, bring me to the nearest psychiatrist and call my dad on the way which will set off a chain reaction of the entire family entering into a downward spiral. I think I'll go the dehydration route. "Mr. Mandley, I didn't have anything to drink today which has obviously led me to become seriously dehydrated and ultimately led to me passing out. I am fine."

"Mr. Mandow, although I appreciate your diagnosis and explanation of the situation, I feel it's best if your mom comes and picks you up so that you can go home and hydrate and get some rest." stated Mr. Mandley. I could tell that the dehydration plan had indeed backfired. Plan B.

"May I go to the bathroom by myself please?" I asked with a hint of sarcasm.

"I think that would be ok. If you need anything, just give me a holler." he stated. I winked and made a B-line for the bathroom. I closed the door, locked it behind me, pretended to lift the toilet seat (sound and all) and then proceeded to text my mom to avert disaster.

I am perfectly fine. Nurse overacting as usual.

I didn't eat or drink yet and I know you told me a hundred times that breakfast is the most important meal of the day.

I was running late this morning. No need for pick up.

I'm going back to class.

I sat down on the toilet and waited for a response. I realized that I had forgotten if I actually put the toilet lid back down but seemed to luck out this time. As I stared down at my cell phone the familiar "someone is responding" bubble came into view on the bottom left hand of my screen. I closed my eyes. Do I dare read her response?

Not happening Peanut!

I'm on my way to you

You are going to come home where I will be making you something to eat

And you're going to drink 8 glasses of water!

I love you.

Oh, no. That was not the text I was hoping for. She was obviously in maternal overload mode and I was screwed. The question not lingering was should I a) try and sneak out of the bathroom past Mr. Mandley and hope Ryan went back to class, b) stay in the bathroom and have a horrible (fake) bought of diarrhea complete with convincing sound effects or c) go home with mom and face the music? If you said c, you are today's lucky winner! The other two options seemed just too risky and time consuming. Better to face my mom, deal with the consequences and enjoy the attention and care only my mom can give me. Maybe that would shake me out of this madness.

I opened the door half expecting to see Ryan standing there with a worried look on his face. Much to my surprise he had gone back to class on the suggestion of Mr. Mandley who was sitting at his desk organizing band-aids by their color and size. I slowly walked over to Mr. Mandley and waited for him to look up. "Christian, you are looking better already. How are you feeling?" Since I had made up my mind to go with option c while in the bathroom, I decided to play the sympathy card a bit.

"I think I should probably lie down and wait for my mom to come just in case I feel dizzy again." I replied.

"Great idea, Chris. Would you like some water or an ice pack?"

"No. I'm really okay. Thanks though."

I went over to the cot and put my head down on the pillow. Mr. Mandley had a thing for homeopathic remedies and as such, the pillows always smelled of lavender. I wasn't sure if he inserted lavender directly into the pillow or if the smell was just a result of some hippie laundry detergent.

Either way, it put me in to a euphoric state which was welcoming after the ordeal I just went through. With every inhale, I felt sleep creeping in and taking hold. What my brain decided to do next was shocking.

Chapter 5
I'm Watching You

~

"What do you mean the boy is not ready to meet his destiny?" a monstrous voice bellowed. A flash of light seemed to illuminate a scene that was both scary and familiar at the same time.

"Master, I have tried to signal him using the bark code and using ink etching and cannot seem to make the signal strong enough to draw him in!" pleaded a small man in the corner.

"You have other means of bringing the boy here. He is mine and I want him in short order!" said the daunting figure. The figure was becoming clearer with every breath I took. He was a large man, brown skin, perhaps of Indian descent and he wore a headdress with a white cloth wrapped around his waist. From the cloth, hung a series of symbols carved out of some type of metal. One of the symbols I immediately recognized as the symbol that I had seen etched in my left arm on the playground.

"Christian, sweetie pie." a loving voice whispered into my ear gently. I slowly opened my eyes and my mom came in to focus. She was stroking my hair like I was five years old again. "Are you okay, honey? I got here as quickly as I could. Are you feeling well enough to stand up?" she said.

"I'm really okay mom. Can we just go home?" I implored. She walked over to the sign out sheet on Mr. Mandley's desk where they exchanged some words that I could not make out. I really didn't care at that point what people were saying about me. I was too busy trying to understand the strange dream I just had. Why is that symbol so foremost in my thoughts. It means nothing to me. Or does it?

The car ride home was exactly what I had imagined it would be. Mom doting on me like I was really sick and me trying to reassure her that I was fine and just severely dehydrated. When we finally got home all I wanted to do was go on the computer and look up the symbol that seemed to be haunting me.

"Sweetie, drink at least these two bottles of water and I am making you something to eat of which you are going to consume at least 75% of." My mom tended to put things into a percentage when she was very serious. I made a b-line to my room and found my dog curled up under the platform bed where she was snoring away. I made my way over to my laptop, plopped down in my chair and began my search for the meaning behind the elusive symbol.

Chapter 6
Meanings

~

As far as I could remember the symbol looked something like this:

I couldn't remember much of what was contained within the symbol glistening on the tree however, I could remember what was etched into my arm and it was exactly the image above. It was almost as if it had been burned into my brain. I pulled up Google and began by entering "Ancient Symbols" in the search bar. I clicked on images and waited for a ridiculous number of pages to load. Upon scrolling through the first few pages, I found nothing that resembled what I had remembered from the symbol on my arm. I continued to search through countless pages of images in hopes that one would pop out at me.

What seemed like two hours later on page 23 of a Google search came the image that had been emblazoned in my recent memory. I stared at it for a moment and then glanced down at the inside of my right forearm almost expecting to see it on my skin. It was not. That was a minor relief. I clicked on the image of the mysterious symbol to try and find out what it meant. It led me to a link that displayed the image in great detail.

My heart began to race. I tried to ignore the immediate rush of blood circulating through my entire body and concentrate on the task at hand. The information contained on the page was broken up into separate aspects of each part of the symbol. I knew immediately that I had stumbled onto something more complicated than I had originally thought. Apparently, there was more to the symbol than just simply resembling an eye. The eye portion was merely one part of a larger sketch of symbolic shapes each holding their own meaning.

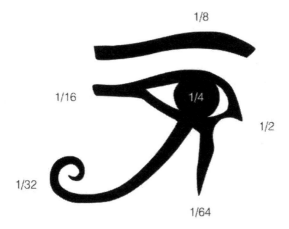

⅛ - representing thought
1/16 - representing hearing
½ - representing sense of smell
1/32 - representing sense of taste
¼ - representing sight
1/64 - representing touch

As informative as this diagram was, it meant absolutely nothing to me. What on Earth could this have to do with me and my life? Perhaps nothing and I was indeed losing my mind. Still, I was mesmerized by the image and their apparent meanings. Every line, every curve, seemed to speak to me with a message I could not yet decode. The yearning to find out how it pertained to my life was certainly stronger than the feeling I had that I could be insane. I decided that if this indeed was real, I needed to find out why this reality had come to be.

Chapter 7
Warmth Returns

~

Tossed and turned that evening trying to dream up an explanation for all of the day's events. I searched every corner of my mind for some deep seeded memory or image that might explain the image, the pain, and the feeling that had come over me that day. As I ventured further into a sleep induced coma, I was carried away into a dream I would soon not forget.

"Why must it be him, Master? Surely there are stronger, more intelligent young men we can pursue." begged a small figure.

"YOU DARE QUESTION MY JUDGEMENT!" bellowed a monstrous voice. At once I recognized the figure as the ancient looking man from my previous day's daydream. I immediately felt sick to my stomach and woke up only to vomit over the side of my bed. What was happening to me? Maybe I was losing my mind after all. I had read about people that were mentally ill and how they were easily able to manifest physical symptoms as a result of their psychosis. That had to be it. I suddenly began to feel lightheaded and called out to my mom. The last thing I could remember about that night is my mom placing a cold cloth on my head and holding my hand. Her warmth radiated throughout my entire body and the dream disappeared.

The next day at school was quite uneventful considering the previous day. The only slightly interesting thing that occurred was that we began our study on Ancient Egypt. During Social Studies I was surprisingly attentive and interested. I guess so much so that Ms. Tincot asked me to stay for a few minutes after the culmination of the lesson and before recess so we could "talk." That usually meant that I was in some sort of trouble but from the pleasant look on her face I thought perhaps my luck had changed. "Christian, are you okay after what happened yesterday?" she said in a gentle tone.

"Yeah, I mean it was a little weird and all but I do feel much better today. I am just hoping that insanity hasn't gotten the best of me." I said half-jokingly.

Ms. Tincot did not seem to find my words half as amusing as I did, and her expression quickly changed from caring to grave concern. "I just want you to know that I know you have had a difficult time in the past with school and teachers but please know that this is a fresh start and anytime you need to talk, I am here."

"Thanks, Ms. Tincot that really means a lot to me and if I knew exactly what I needed to talk about I would tell you. I'm not sure what happened or why it happened, but I am determined to find out one way or another. I can't stand watching my mom become sick with worry." I said.

"That statement is exactly why I like you Christian. You have a good heart." she said with a smile. "Have a great lunch. Oh, by the way, it seems like you have a real affinity for Ancient Egypt. Have you read a lot about the civilization prior to us beginning our lessons?"

"I don't think so" I retorted. " I just seem to know about everything you're teaching us pertaining to Ancient Egypt."

That statement to Ms. Tincot stayed with me throughout lunch and recess. How did I know everything she was lecturing about? I had never picked up a single book on Ancient Egyptian culture nor had I ever even watched a special about it on the History Channel. It made no sense. So much for an uneventful day at school.

I got off of the bus that afternoon still thinking about Ms. Tincot's lesson. She began the lesson by teaching us about the importance of gods and goddesses in Ancient Egypt. One of the goddesses she taught about was Maat. As soon as she said the name, I felt a warmth that usually only comes over me when I am around my mother. Odd. Maat was the goddess of truth and wisdom and controlled the seasons and the movement of the stars. I knew this although how I'm not sure.

That night, I stared out my window while having great difficulty getting to sleep. Upon gazing out my window, I noticed some stars that seemed to be aligned in an odd pattern. I quickly got out of bed and walked over to the window and looked up into the night sky. What I saw next sent chills down my spine. The stars seemed to be forming words. Those words read, "CHRISTIAN, FEAR NOT. YOU ARE THE CHOSEN ONE."

I blinked several times, looked away from the window and then looked back up at the sky again hoping that the stars had taken a different form. They had not.

Chapter 8
A Walk to Remember

~

I think I hit snooze a hundred times before finally falling out of bed that morning. The only decent thing about waking up today is that it was Saturday. That meant there could be no possibility of strange things happening at school that might further embarrass me. Everything at home had been somewhat normal and status quo that morning. The only abnormal events had been my dreams and the writing in the sky formed by stars. They were only dreams I kept telling myself in hopes that I would somehow convince myself that that indeed was the case.

"Christian, honey, hurry up and get dressed. We are going to go to the trail for a walk. It'll be good for everyone mentally and physically." yelled my mom. "I'm not even...." I started but was abruptly silenced. "You're not even nothing! Get dressed!" she replied. I just love when my mother gets on these "family togetherness" kicks. It usually means that we will have to venture into the tick laden woods in search of some peaceful balance in order to realign our chakras. The idea of walking for miles with my mom and dad in search of alignment was not particularly peaceful. I got dressed, grabbed a protein bar and conceded.

"Mom, is there a reason we need to start the weekend off by walking in the woods instead of relaxing in front of perhaps...a computer?" I said.

"Um...hmmm... let me see. Yes, it's called fresh air, clearing our heads, and actually becoming one with nature." she said. Here we go, I thought. Tonight's dinner will be some sort of white fish and kale. Oh boy, perhaps being insane at school was not as bad an option as I had originally thought.

It was nearly 11am and there we were walking along the path that led through a forest off of the main trail when I felt a familiar tingling on my arm. I looked down at my arm expecting to see the symbol. It was not there. I was probably imagining the sensation. As I walked behind my mom and dad, I looked up at the trees, the highest branches intermingling with one another against a backdrop of a perfectly azure sky. I actually felt calmer and had an inner peace that I had not felt in a long time. I was not going to express that to my mother though.

I sat down on a large rock and continued to gaze skyward. The clouds were few and far between and they seemed to be coming in and out of view through the tangles of branches. Perhaps I was more like my mom than I had originally thought. Although I can't ever see myself becoming CEO of "Green You" her environmentally conscious cleaning product company. Sure, she makes fairly good money but at the expense of driving others crazy with her obsessive environmental issues.

I closed my eyes for a moment to drink in the peace and solitude only to open them to an alarming sight. The branch formations that had no definitive pattern previously, had now formed an obvious shape. Their thin branches spelling out words that sent chills through my entire body. I tried to scream to my mom and dad but could not get one vocal cord to work. I sat with my mouth gaping open like a bass and no sound came out. I tried to focus all of my energy into creating a sound that would alert my parents. I could hear nothing but the gently blowing of the wind, the trees mocking me with their message, and my body frozen in time. "YOU CANNOT ESCAPE WHAT IS DESTINED TO BE. FEAR NOT AND SURRENDER." The branches had formed these horrific words and I could not speak.

I was unable to move, unable to speak, just staring at the branches in fear. Ok, I thought to myself, this is just a symptom of whatever mental illness I had succumbed to. I decided to close my eyes and try to reorient myself in hopes of changing my current situation. I assumed that I had fallen asleep due to the fact that it felt as if I were in a dream like state. "You are one difficult man to entice into the Netherworld" echoed a deep, familiar voice.

Once again, I tried to speak but no sound left my lips. Can one hear themselves speak in a dream I wondered? While I was contemplating this I realized that I was gaining some sensation throughout parts of my body.

I decided I had had enough of these visions speaking only to each other and never to me.

"Explain yourselves!" I screamed. It was the first time I had heard my own voice and been able to utter sounds since the message appeared in the trees.

"Master, would you like me to silence him?" asked a small shadowy figure.

"How many times must I explain to you that when I want something, I WILL ASK YOU? You are not to think for yourself until further notice!"

"Yes, master." the frightened figure replied.

"I really have no time for your games or your willful denial of the situation that has been presented to you." growled the figure. "It will do you no good to scream at us, threaten us or try to resist at this point. We will only draw you back in." stated the figure.

"Back in to what?" I pleaded. "I have absolutely no idea why I am having this dream in the first place or what any of it means!"

"All I can tell you is right now is that it is far from a dream my boy. It is your alternate reality. One in which you must get used to traveling in and out of in order to meet your destiny." the massive figure stated.

"Who are you?" I begged.

"I am Osiris. God of the dead. Do you not recognize a member of your own family?" bellowed the figure.

"My family?" I stammered. "That isn't really possible considering I have a mom and dad I know very well back in my 'other reality' and they are far from Ancient Egyptian gods. Thank you for the invite though."

"It is not a choice boy! Your tongue may be sharp but let us see if your mind can match the sharpness of your tongue and the daunting tasks ahead of you." he said.

At that moment, I decided to look down at my arm for some reason and there, in all of its glory was the elusive symbol I had scoured the internet trying to learn more about. It looked slightly different this time. Instead of pure black, the edges of each part of the symbol glowed with a golden hue. I stared at it for what seemed like an eternity until a sudden warm rush came over my body and carried me away from what I imagined was a dream.

Chapter 9
Why Me?

~

"Mom, it doesn't feel like a dream." I insisted. Her eyes seemed to be mixed with conflicting emotions. She stared at me for what seemed like an eternity with a mixture of compassion and confusion.

"Honey, I understand. I have had dreams in which I really feel as if they are actually happening." she implored.

"It can be disconcerting and disorienting, but it doesn't mean that you are going crazy or that you are mentally unstable as you seem to be convinced of."

She was clearly having difficulty understanding the intensity of these dreams and visions. I could certainly understand how she would be unable to comprehend the intensity and realistic nature of my "dreams." Even I had difficulty telling whether I had actually been awake or asleep during these times. For a moment, I felt terribly alone and scared. It was as if a huge weight had been placed on my shoulders and I wasn't even sure what the weight was from.

As usual, that morning I met up with Ryan at the bus stop and we discussed the usual weekend happenings along with the fact that we both hated Mondays' more than anything. Ryan seemed to act normally towards me after all that had happened, which was comforting considering all that had occurred over the past week. I decided not to tell Ryan about the dreams that I had been having over the past few days for fear that he might change his mind about being friends with me. I wanted him to believe that I had some minor assemblance of sanity left.

As we found our seat next to each other on the bus, I saw Ryan glance over at my arm and then quickly look away and out the window. Did he actually see the symbol that had been so clearly etched in my arm that day? I closed my eyes, took a deep breath and looked down at the inside of my arm. No symbol. "Ryan, I know this sounds crazy but, just amuse me here. Were you just looking over at my arm to see if there was something strange on it?" I said.

"Why on Earth would I be looking at your arm?" he said in an uneasy manner.

"Well... I... uh... no reason. Sorry." I stammered. I quickly changed the subject to the video game we had been playing online last night and Ryan soon recovered from my strange line of questioning.

As the bus rounded the corner, Ryan commented that he had a terrible night's sleep and closed his eyes as we turned into the bus circle and began the roller coaster of speed bumps. I stared at the back seat in front of me and my eyes began going in and out of focus. I guess my visions last night had left me tired as well. I noted that there was not a bit of writing on the back of the seat which was highly unusual considering every other seat we sat in on the bus was littered with graffiti that usually made no sense, was misspelled, and not even the slightest bit interesting to read. As we hit the last speed bump and approached the front of the school, my vision became disturbingly clear and what I saw was bone-chilling.

It looked like it had been written using a marker just like most of the graffiti I had seen on the bus for years, only this graffiti sent a shiver down my spine. I grabbed Ryan's arm and pointed at the seat.

"Hey, man, what are you doing?" he said in an annoyed tone pulling his arm away from me.

"Don't you see this drawing on the seat?" I pleaded. "Please tell me you see this!" I yelled.

"Christian... I'm sorry. I don't see anything." he said a note of concern in his voice.

I looked away from Ryan and back at the symbol. All I could think of at that point was "Why me?" Why was this happening to me? Maybe I had had some sort of seizure that made me see things that weren't really there. Maybe it is some medical condition that the doctors were unaware of or had yet to discover. The bus came to an abrupt stop as we reached the front door. I remained fixed on the symbol until Ryan said "Chris, man, we need to get off. Do you want me to walk to the nurse with you?" I looked at him confused and too frightened to speak. We got off the bus and it was off to Mr. Mandley, again.

Chapter 10
The Infirmary, Again.

~

"Back again, Christian!" the nurse said in a sarcastic tone. I looked over at Ryan pleading for his silence about what had happened on the bus.

"Um… yeah… well, Chris had a really bad headache and I didn't want him to walk here alone." stated Ryan.

"Okay, Let's take your temperature, shall we?" stated Mr. Mandley emphatically.

I sat there on the all too familiar lavender scented cot with the thermometer under my tongue. My heart began to race as I thought about the symbol that appeared on the back of the seat on the bus. Another symbol I needed to investigate when I got home. It seemed as if my research had become never-ending. All I could think about while sitting there was what did the mysterious symbol mean and how long would it be until I could get to a computer to Google it? "Let's check that temp shall we?" Mr. Mandley stated. I tried not to look him in the eye for fear of him asking me more questions about why I was actually here. "Well, I don't think we need to call an ambulance, but it is slightly elevated." he said. "Do you want to stick it out a bit and come back if you're still not feeling well or should I call mom?" he questioned.

"I'll be okay." I replied. "I didn't eat anything this morning and I had a headache when I woke up so...."

"Mr. Christian, how many times have I told you that breakfast is the most important meal of the day?" he said in a sing-song tone.

As I got up to leave to go to class, I started conjuring up my plan to stop at the computer lab on the way to class in order to begin my search for the symbol. I knew it was risky considering I was already late to class and if I got caught it might mean a detention. I decided to risk it of course.

I slipped into the dark computer lab, but not before checking the sign-up sheet to see if a class was going to come in soon. It appeared that I was safe until around 10:15. I looked down at my watch, 9:40. I had enough time to log-on, search, and print. I entered my username and password on a computer tucked in the corner of the room. It seemed to take forever to load, but once it did, I typed Google into the search bar and began my crusade. I chuckled to myself for a moment when I actually thought about what on Earth people did before Google. I wasn't sure how to go about searching for the symbol considering I knew nothing of its origin and had absolutely no idea what it even meant. I went for the obvious search on symbols of Ancient Egypt. I clicked on images... it was the first image I found. I thought, what were the chances of that.

I stared at it for what seemed like an eternity realizing it wasn't actually one symbol but a collection. Still, I was no closer to understanding why I had seen it on the bus. I clicked on the image hoping to be redirected to a website that might give me some more information. Unfortunately, as my luck would have it, it brought me to a larger, more detailed picture of the same graphic. Devoid of any meaning. There were several paragraphs on Ancient Egypt and what some symbols meant to the Egyptians but nothing that led me to the ultimate meaning of the actual image. I quickly looked down at my watch and realized that it was coming up on 10:10 which made me a bit nervous considering I knew a class was scheduled at 10:15. I quickly pressed print and shut down the computer. I grabbed the sheet from the printer and headed out the door to class.

"Woah, there cowboy! Where are you off too in such a hurry?" stated a voice that had become all too familiar to me.

"Oh, Mr. Martin, hi. Isn't it a beautiful day today?" I said in my best student voice.

"Yes, it is. However, I'd like to know why on this beautiful day you are exiting the computer lab sans your class?" he said.

"I um... Well... okay, I'll be honest. I know you respect my honesty, so here it goes.   I forgot to print out my research paper and it is due today, so I took a bit of a detour." I said in a matter of fact tone.

"I would love nothing more than to take a look at your paper if you don't mind." he said in a sarcastic tone. "You know I have always been a big fan of your writing style."

"Right. Well. I would hate for you to see it when it isn't complete, so I'll do some editing during social studies and bring it to your office later." I said nervously.

"I'm sure the rough draft is a great read." he said, "So I'll take it now."

I handed over the only paper in my hand which held the elusive symbol. He stared at it for what seemed like hours, looked up at me, then back at the paper, then back up at me again. I thought perhaps I had printed out a different picture, one that was inappropriate or perhaps a string of curse words the way he was staring at me. The look of a very confused principal.

"This doesn't seem to be quite a research paper, does it?" he said

"Yeah, well I told you it definitely needs some work." I said without thinking.

"You can finish it during lunch when you are serving detention." he said in an angry tone. "Now, get to class!"

I could have predicted this would happen considering it is not unusual for me to get caught doing things I shouldn't be doing. I was almost tempted to tell him about the events of the past week and how this symbol showed up on the back of the bus seat today but thought better of it. I'm glad I didn't open my mouth since he already thought I was trouble. Here's to another eventful school day.

Chapter 11
The Rest of the Day

~

I arrived in class on the late side. Okay, an hour late. "Hey, Christian, is everything ok?" stated Ms. Tincot. I had a feeling this lady might actually care a bit about me. I knew that if I let my guard down though it would get me into trouble with her eventually. I looked around for Ryan and found him towards the back of the classroom almost looking frightened to see me. I plopped down into the empty seat next to him and gave him a slightly reassuring smile.

"Okay, so today's lesson is about the ancient system of hieroglyphics so vital to the Ancient Egyptian civilization." said Ms. Tincot.

Those words so seemingly harmless sent a shiver down my spine. I started to become extremely anxious and fidgeted in my seat almost uncontrollably. Ryan looked over concerned and whispered, "Are you okay man?" I mouthed back that I was okay, and the lesson continued.

"So, in studying this ancient language we see many symbols showing up over and over again that actually have very significant meanings and can be the key to understanding everyday Ancient Egyptian life" Ms. Tincot remarked. I realized that I had yet to take out a notebook and pen and figured that might be a good idea considering I was an hour late to class. I reached into my desk and pulled out my social studies notebook and fumbled for a pen. Ms. Tincot began to put a series of hieroglyphics on the board just as I put pen to paper.

I began to draw each symbol almost instinctively. I looked down and tried to ignore the fact that I had just

filled the entire page with hieroglyphics
and when I glanced at them, they all
made perfect sense to me.

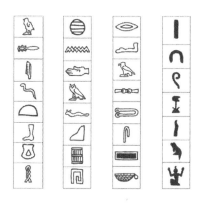

Ryan leaned over and whispered
to me, which broke my fixation on the
hieroglyphs I had just drawn in my
notebook. "Hey, Chris, what does the
arrow mean underneath all of the
hieroglyphics? That's not on the board
but you drew it." I looked up at the
whiteboard hoping to see an arrow
drawn under the hieroglyphics Ms.
Tincot had copied. No arrow. I looked
over at Ryan who was patiently waiting
for an answer. I leaned over and

whispered, "I don't know.....I just felt it belonged there."

Ryan gave me a confused look, shook his head, and went back to listening to the lecture and copying from the board. I started to get lost in what was on my paper. So much so that I no longer heard anything Ms. Tincot said. While I was examining the shapes on my paper trying to decipher what they meant, the mysterious arrow had suddenly begun to glow. I stared at it and then tried my hardest to pull my fixed gaze away and refocus. I could not. I couldn't look away from the arrow on the paper. In my head, I kept repeating, "This is not happening. It is in your head. A manifestation of your apparent panic disorder."

When I was finally able to lift my gaze, I looked over at the computers where the arrow seemed to be pointing and there on the screen, were these words.

Christian...

**You MUST STOP trying to deny the power that is within you. The Master will win! It is imperative that you come with me now.
Your life as you know it is about to change forever...**

I continued to stare at the computer in disbelief and looked over at Ryan to bring his attention to the words on the screen. Ryan was not there. I looked around. NO one was there. I was alone with the words on the screen. I looked back at the computer and started to get up from my desk when I felt a presence behind me. Petrified to turn around, I made the executive decision to ignore the feeling.

"You cannot hide forever, Christian. It is your fate and inevitably it will take hold. You will have no choice but to give in." said a low booming voice. I turned to see the figure that had been so prevalent in my dreams over the past few months. When I tried to speak, no words left my lips. "You are not permitted to speak at this point. I have taken care of that by silencing you." he said. "I want you to simply listen to what I have to say." I stared at him with a strange sense of relief and gratitude. Why did I feel so connected to something that I should be frightened of? The feeling was similar to when my mother comforted me.

This where it all ended, and it all began.

Chapter 12
Silence

~

Not being one to follow directions, I tried to speak. No sound came. The figure looked at me mockingly and made a gesture to his throat. "Strange feeling isn't it? Not being able to utter a single word. Especially for a boy who has no problem figuring out a quick and witty remark." the figure said. It was frustrating and strange. I thought better of opening my mouth following those words. "So, Christian, I realize this may be somewhat out of the ordinary. I can very much assure you that this is not a dream or a figment of your very overactive imagination. It is real and incredibly important. So, listen carefully."

He began by explaining why he had chosen me and what that meant.

The words were strange and distant as if in a dream. I began to bite my tongue, hard, to see if I was in fact dreaming. It hurt and began to bleed a bit the metallic taste of blood filling my mouth. This was no dream. Perhaps I should look for some sort of an escape. I glanced around the room. The door that was usually the entrance to our classroom was mysteriously replaced by a continuation of the wall. I quickly glanced behind me where there usually resides another door. Just a wall again. This was really happening.

"So," the mysterious figure continued. "As you can see, you are the only one who can complete this task successfully. I would say the choice is yours however, it is not. The choice is mine and as such, you will bring me the components contained in the Eye of Horus by the weeks end." I had lost track of what he was saying halfway through worrying about finding a way out. Since I could not reply, I decided it best to nod acknowledging the order I was given. He seemed pleased for the first time with my response. I took a breath and closed my eyes for what seemed like a split second. When I opened them, things were as they had been before this vision.

"Hey, man, pay attention. She didn't even draw that crazy arrow that's taking up half of your page. You're going to get in trouble again." stated Ryan. I had sketched a picture of the Eye of Horus on my paper. It seemed to be glaring back at me knowingly. I looked up at Ryan in disbelief. "What the heck, why are you staring at me like that?" I yelled. The bell rang signaling recess and I couldn't move.

"Are you okay, Christian?" said Ms. Tincot. I looked up and begged her to tell me that I had fallen asleep in class. "Christian, now you know I would have thrown something at you if you had." she said sarcastically. I managed to muster a faint smile, put my books in my desk, and walk out to the field. Ryan was outside talking to some of our friends when I approached, he looked over ending his conversation. "I know. I've been acting like a crazy idiot. Can we talk? Somewhere private?" The group looked at me strangely and walked away. Ryan and I walked over to the infamous tree that bore the strange symbol. I hoped that the tree would help me explain things to Ryan in a way he could understand. He stood silently looking at me, waiting for an explanation.

I began to tell him everything, from the time I saw the strange symbol on the tree until this afternoon when I had been visited once again by the mysterious figure. Ryan was silent for what seemed like an eternity. I was hoping his silence was the result of him trying to comprehend what he had just been told. It turns out I was half right. "Chris, you are my best friend. You are like a brother to me and because of that, I am going to implore you to get some help." he said. He was right of course; I did need help. Just not the kind he was suggesting.

Chapter 13
Touch

~

I walked through the front door and was met with the smell of my dad's delicious cooking. It was comforting and made me feel somewhat better about the events of the day. I took the opportunity to try and talk to my dad alone for a while. "Hey dad, is mom home yet?" I said. He shook his head no and continued to stir the dinner. "Dad, that smells amazing. What kind of chili is it?" I asked.

"It's actually not chili. It's a dish called Koshari." he replied. "I don't even remember where I learned to make it.

Must have picked it up on my travels somewhere." I was immediately distracted by what he had just told me and had a hard time recovering. For some reason, the dish sounded oddly familiar. But how could it?

"Um, yeah. I actually have a ton of homework, so I'll come back in a bit." I said. I took off to my room and looked up Koshari. It was an Ancient Egyptian recipe. What the hell was going on? I laid down on my bed to contemplate the day's events and no sooner had my head hit the pillow and I was asleep.

"Christian... Christian..." whispered a voice. I woke up with a start expecting to see the looming figure above me. I was relieved to see my mother standing there with a look of concern on her face. "Honey, dad said you seemed like something was bothering you when you came home. Do you want to talk?" she said in a comforting tone.

"Why is dad making Koshari?" I blurted out.

She chuckled, smiled at me, and stroked the hair out of my face. "Because that's what he chose to make tonight. If you don't like it, I'll make you something else." she said. I stared back at her frustrated that she had no idea what was behind that question. She grabbed my hand, turned it over so that my palm was facing up and placed a long slender stick across it.

"What is this?" I uttered. She explained that someone she worked with had been traveling in Europe and purchased it from a street fair. Supposedly, it was a "power stick". It could give one the power to control their fate. As she was explaining where it came from, I could feel my heart beating faster and faster and I became nauseous. I looked at her with sheer panic and began to hyperventilate.

"Honey, calm down!" she exclaimed. The next thing I knew, I was in a hospital bed with wires coming out of my arms. The only thing I could feel was the touch of my mother with one hand on my forehead and the other clutching my right hand tightly. I found a moment of comfort in this sensation and then all went black.

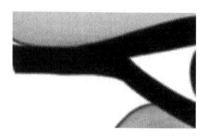

All I could hear upon gaining consciousness was the hum of machines and the voice of my mother speaking softly. "Christian, honey, how do you feel?" I honestly felt as if I had been hit by a Mack truck but wouldn't dare tell her that. She gently stroked my hand and it was pulling me back into a dream like state. "Mom, I'm tired, but I'm really fine." I said.

I looked around at the hospital room and realized that I must have been there for quite a while considering there were some flowers on the table. "Mom, what happened?" I whispered. "Oh, honey, you don't remember. You just blacked out again. They are going to run some tests and we are going to get to the bottom of this I promise." she said in a comforting tone. I listened to the machines making various beeping noises and heard the song of the distant birds outside of the window that light was streaming through. It hurt my eyes to look out of the window, so I quickly averted them back to my mother. "I'm going to go see if I can find the doctor who is going to run the EEG. Will you be ok for a few minutes?" she said. I nodded reassuringly and my mom left the room.

While I was alone, I couldn't help but look out the window and wonder why all of this was happening. Maybe the EEG would show some sign of abnormal brain wave patterns and this would all be explained. The prospect of something showing up in the test both excited and frightened me. I looked over at the table by the window where some flowers had been placed. Why was I receiving flowers already? Unless my mom had brought them in to lend a more balanced chi to the room. I decided that must be where they came from.

As I stared at the petals on the lilies that poked out of the vase, I began to see the petals glow. No, it was a trick of the sunlight. Petals don't glow! As soon as this thought came to mind, I sensed a strange smell, like incense only terribly strong. This was not just the cheap incense in the cones my mom had lying around and sometimes burned to "clear" the energy. This was a distinct smell that seemed oddly familiar. As I took in the calming smell with each breath, I realized there was a swirl of smoke forming in front of my face. I looked over at the lilies. It seemed to be emanating from each petal of the flower. As I watched in amazement, each petal let of a swirl of smoke that seemed to flow directly in front of my face. The smoke swirled around me and formed the words that I will never forget.

WE NEED YOU NOW!

YOUR FATE IS SEALED.

THE NEXT VISION WILL BE YOUR TIME FOR ACTION.

Surely, I must be imagining the words in the smoke. It must have been like when you look at clouds and they seem to be forming some sort of a shape, like an animal or inanimate object.

As the smoke swirled, I felt a sense of well-being come over me and tingling all through my body. I tried to speak but could only whisper the words, "I will accept my fate and join the crusade."

"I am elated that you have finally come to your senses" a familiar voice said. I was quickly shaken out of this state as the doctor entered the room.

"Are you ready for your EEG, Christian?" stated the doctor.

What would they find?

Chapter 15
Sight

~

With wires dangling out of my head, I was hooked up to a monitor that seemed to be recording my brain waves. As I stared at the monitor, I was mesmerized by the different colored lines. "What is this going to tell us?" I asked the doctor.

"Well, Christian, if you have had or are having any seizures, it will let us know." he said. Could this be the explanation for all that was happening to me? I wasn't so sure. As the lines blipped across the screen, I couldn't help but wonder how it actually worked. I had never been one for medical information. My mom looked on anxiously. "Okay, so we are going to start. You will see a series of flashing lights when I put this mask on you. Try not to move. You will also need to listen to my directions as I am going to ask you to take short deep breaths at some point during the test." stated the doctor. I was getting a bit anxious as I never experienced something like this before. I took a deep breath and decided that if there was a real possibility that I was experiencing all of this because of seizures, I would have to work through the anxiety and take the test.

The lights began to flash and whirl around my eyes dancing in various colors. Although it was a bit annoying, I actually found the lights to be somewhat therapeutic. I became a bit sleepy but fought the temptation to take a snooze. As the lights flashed, I began to see an image of a man that had become all too familiar to me. It was Maat. He was not

happy. "What is it going to take to draw you in, boy!" he bellowed. "Perhaps this test is what we needed all along."
I resisted the temptation to open my eyes for fear that it might cause the test to be inconclusive. I focused on the man before me.

"Why are you so determined to talk to me!" I screamed in my head.

"Because you are the chosen one. The one boy who can figure out the ultimate mystery." he said.

What mystery that was was still beyond me. "I have no power that I know of." I thought to myself.

"That is not true. You have the ultimate power. The power to see all sides of a problem and work out the solution." he retorted. "You can solve the mystery that has been plaguing us for centuries."

I had no idea what he was talking about but I have to admit, I was intrigued by his statement. As the lights swirled in my vision and Maat spoke, I could hear another voice that brought me slowly back to reality. It was the voice of my mother telling me that there were only a few minutes left in the test. I was relieved and disappointed at the same time.

In my head I said, "Maat, what is the mystery you are talking about and how do I help solve it?" He let out a low, deep chuckle and pointed his staff directly at me. In that moment, it became clear that I had a destiny to fulfill.

Chapter 16
Smell

~

Burning. Burning wires. That was the smell that accompanied my mother's voice. Why was I smelling burning wires? That could not be a good sign. "Mom, mom!" I yelled. "What is that burning smell!"

"Sweetheart, there is no smell, I promise." she said reassuringly. I could have sworn I smelled something burning. I touched my head to see if my hair was burning and felt only the soft puff of hair that was usually on top of my head. It didn't seem crispy, so I figured I was safe there. I looked down at the wires once the doctor had removed the mask and saw no sign of smoke or melted plastic. I didn't understand. I know I smelled burning and it seemed as if it were an electrical smell coupled with some sort of spicy smell. Made no sense. The doctor removed the wires from my head and the smell dissipated.

"Okay, Christian, you're all done. We should have results in a few days." he stated. A few days! A lot can happen to me in a few days, I thought. As the doctor used a wipe to clean up the sticky substance where the electrodes had been adhered to my head, I sensed the strange odor again. It wasn't as strong as the first time, but still apparent.

"Mom, seriously, do you not smell that?"

"Honey, I do not. I believe that you think you smell it but it could just be a trick of your very vivid imagination or maybe it's the gel the doctor used." she said in a comforting tone. Either way, it was there, and it was real.

The car ride home was uneventful, at least in my world. I could still see the flashing lights faintly in my vision but other than that, all was quiet. No visions, no words in the sky, no swirling smoke. Just my mom singing to Queen playing on the radio and me picking the last bits of gel from my hair. When we arrived home, my dad was waiting for us in the driveway. "Hey, buddy, how are you feeling?" he said.

"I'm okay dad. Just had a brain wave examination complete with stinky gel and wires and we are waiting to see if I actually have a brain. So, yeah, there's that." I said sarcastically.

"I'm sorry I wasn't able to get to the hospital in time. Traffic was a mess on the expressway coming back from work and mom said I should just meet you back at home." he said.

"It's cool dad. I'm fine." I reassured him.

Once inside, I made a dash for my bedroom and mom yelled that she would bring me something to drink and start making dinner. I wasn't really hungry but felt I probably should keep that to myself for fear that my mom might worry about my lack of hunger as well as my brain waves.

I plopped down on my bed and closed my eyes for a moment to see if the lights would still be swirling around my vision. They were not. It seemed as if that phenomenon had died down and perhaps there was something to this seizure thing. I started breathing heavily and the rhythm of my breath sounds put me in to a catatonic state. I felt almost euphoric.

"The mystery is one that is as Ancient as I am." he stated. "It is one that has eluded many for centuries. Many great people before you have tried to piece together the mystery of Tut to no avail." Tut! Was this vision out of his mind? Or was I. I fixed my gaze upon Maat and tried to get him to tell me more. He vanished.

Chapter 17
Taste

~

"Honey, dinner!" bellowed my mom. It had been about an hour from what I could tell since I had fallen into a deep slumber and had my last visit from Maat. All I could think about was what he had told me and how I needed to conduct some research on the mystery of King Tut.

"Mom, what do you know about King Tut?" I said.

"Well, he was only a boy when he became King, he married his half-sister, and he loved ostrich hunting. I also believe he had some sort of issue with his feet and as a result, had to wear an orthopedic type sandal." she said in a surprised tone.

"Mom, that's a lot of weird facts. How do you even know any of that?" I said.

"I have absolutely no idea." she stammered. My dad looked very confused and shook his head.

"Your mom is an encyclopedia, my boy. It amazes me some of the strange historical facts she knows." he said.

My mother was silent throughout the remainder of dinner. I however could not stop asking questions about the boy king and decided that research needed to commence immediately after dinner. "Can I be excused?" I said in a rushed tone.

"Um... clean up your plate." my dad said. I brought my dish to the kitchen and loaded it in the dishwasher. Upon opening the dishwasher, that familiar spicy smell welled up in my nostrils again.

"Mom, mom, I can smell that weird smell again." I yelled. My mom came into the kitchen and said she could smell nothing. Just as those words left her lips, I began to sense a rather metallic taste on my tongue. I stuck my tongue out and crossed my eyes to see if I could tell if it was bleeding. I didn't see any blood. I carefully touched my finger to the tip of my tongue and nothing. The taste suddenly changed to that of eating a raw onion and I took my fingers and started wiping my tongue frantically.

"Honey, come quick, I think Christian is having a seizure!" my mom yelled out to my dad in the dining room. My dad stumbled into the kitchen and looked at me concerned.

"No, dad, I'm ok. I just had a weird taste in my mouth." I said. "I'm sure it was just something from dinner."
I made my way up to my room and could hear the muffled sounds of conversation between my mom and dad. My mother was going on and on about how she really felt as if seizures were to blame and my dad was trying to console her by saying that they shouldn't jump to any conclusions. I listened for a while and soon fell asleep.

During my slumber, Maat and his servant came to visit. They were both a bit more pleasant this time. "Boy, if you give in and come with us, you will find that your life will be more balanced, and the truth will become clear. Your destiny is to solve the greatest mystery ever to have graced this Earth. The mystery of King Tut's early demise." he stated. "Do you accept this challenge, or must we take you by force?"

I needed to think about this a bit. I had yet to have the opportunity to research the actual mystery and I had no idea what I was even up against.
"I know nothing about King Tut and I really would be of no use to you." I said.

"Silence. That is nonsense. I will not have you spewing such ridiculous claims." he said. At that moment, I knew something was happening and I was about to find out what my role would be in this ultimate quest to solve the mystery of the death of the boy King.

Chapter 17
The Boy King

~

What on Earth did I even know about King Tutankhamen? Not much except what my mother had told me which was just a series of random and rather odd facts. I think she was still reeling from the surprise of blurting those out and not having a clue where they came from. It took me a while to return from my last visit with Maat but when I did, I got to work on researching the mystery I was supposedly destined to solve. I began by searching up "King Tut Murder" and proceeded to click on several links that described in detail the possible ways in which Tut died. As I clicked on each one, I began to imagine what it must have been like to be a boy turned King. There were three theories that kept coming up repeatedly. Each one more interesting and plausible than the next. I was intrigued.

The first theory that came up in my research was that Tut had been injured in battle. While riding his chariot, another warrior attacked him with a spear, puncturing his leg and breaking the tibia. It went on to describe how this led to him becoming extremely sick with gangrene and ultimately dying. It was an interesting theory, but I needed to find out all possibilities before Maat paid me another visit, so I moved on.

The second theory I hit upon was one in which the boy King was hunting and had been in a crash while riding his chariot. This theory suggested that he fell from the chariot and suffered a blow to the head from which he never recovered. Possible.

The third theory spoke of an intentional blow to the head by one of his servants or perhaps some type of enemy. There seemed to be a good amount of evidence to support this theory considering the findings of a CT scan that had been done by modern day archeologists. Just as I began to read the last sentence pertaining to the theory, a video popped up on my screen. I assumed it would be a video depicting the theories of his death that I had just been reading about but much to my surprise, it was Maat.

"So, I see you are accepting what is meant to be and beginning your journey to the Netherworld." he said. "I will assist you in any way that I can, but I need you to trust me implicitly."

"I must admit, as scared as I am, I am intrigued by this mystery" I said. "I am frightened to join you on this journey, but I feel that it is inescapable at this point" I stammered. As I spoke these words, I realized that it didn't even sound like me. It sounded very formal, no hint of sarcasm at all. Very strange, I thought.

"Take my staff and we will begin" he commanded.

"Will I ever come back? What about my mom and dad?" I said in a concerned tone.

"You will be traveling back and forth between the two worlds my boy. While you are in my world, time will stand still in yours so there is no need to worry," he said. No need to worry. I felt as if my heart was going to beat out of my chest. The urge to grab the staff was too strong to ignore and I reached out for the golden rod. Just as I was about to take hold, a flash of light blinded me, and I had to close my eyes.

When I finally opened them, I realized that I was no longer in my bedroom but in a dimly lit room with stone walls. Where was I? I shut my eyes tightly, shook my head and opened them again praying that this was all a bad dream. It was not. There before me, stood Maat and his servant with a look of victory on their faces. "My boy, it is time to begin your investigation in my world. You are the only one who can solve this mystery. Time is of the essence and we can waste not a minute more," he said.

"Where... d-do I... begin?" I stammered.

"You begin at the beginning my boy. You begin by joining me down in Tut's tomb in order to learn all that you can regarding the great King. Are you ready?" he questioned.

I did not know if I was indeed ready, but I was certainly intrigued and there was no turning back now. The journey had begun...

TO BE CONTINUED...

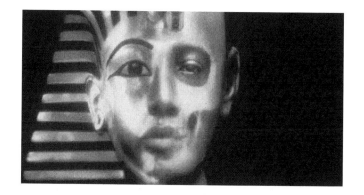

Made in the USA
San Bernardino, CA
25 June 2020